A
Country
Christmas

by Bonnie Lou Risby
Cover illustration by Dan Andreasen

D0167943

SCHOLASTIC INC.

New York Toronto London Auckland Sydney
Mexico City New Delhi Hong Kong Buenos Aires

For Robby . . .
and his grandparents:
Maxine and Jack
and
Mary and Lloyd
whose patchwork of colorful memories forms the
backdrop to all of tomorrow's adventures.

ISBN 0-439-79377-7

12 11 10 9 8 7 6 5 4 3 2   5 6 7 8 9 10/0

Printed in the U.S.A.   40

First Scholastic printing, November 2005

Chapter 1

"What a fellowship, What a joy divine . . ." Francy Ponder stood outside the sewing-room door, listening to her mother's sweet singing. "Leaning, leaning, safe and secure from all alarms. Leaning leaning, leaning on the everlasting arms."

Quietly, Francy opened the door and took the broom from the corner. Her mother smiled as Francy began tidying up the threads and tiny cloth scraps from the floor.

"Thanks, honey," said Mrs. Ponder in a soft drawl. "I guess I'd get lost in here 'cept for you."

This was Francy's favorite room. Here her mother was always the happiest, and that happiness spilled over into songs. Francy and her mother hummed their favorite hymn together as they focused on their tasks.

Mae Ponder was known for miles around as a wizard with a needle and thread. Francy thought her

3

mother's old sewing machine was like the fairy-tale spinning wheel that turned straw into gold. Ever since Francy could remember, her mother had spent her days tailoring slipcovers and draperies for the few rich folk in town. But like so many jobs, that work was disappearing now, too.

Most of Mrs. Ponder's work was making and altering clothing. In return, she received old clothes to remake for her own family. For a time, she had helped Mrs. Trundle at the boarding house, preparing and serving the large noonday meals. But all that had changed. The company that had supplied countless railroad ties had closed, and the gravel company had also moved. The boarding house was never full anymore, so Mrs. Ponder's help was needed only on Saturdays.

The sewing continued in the small room in the big rock house that Francy's father had built for his family in the Ozark hills. Francy never realized how lucky she was to live in such a beautiful place, for she had never been anywhere else. She had no idea that in other parts of the world girls couldn't tell the difference between a dogwood tree and a sassafras tree.

"Let's sing something else," Francy said, sweeping an enormous tangle of blue, yellow, and green threads onto a piece of newspaper.

"What would you like?" her mother asked, never lifting her eyes from the needle.

Francy thought. Her mother knew hundreds of songs, and could call them up as easily as most people say "Howdy." Francy climbed onto the bale of fluffy cotton in the corner that Mrs. Ponder used to stuff pillows. "How about 'Barbara Allen'?"

Her mother sighed. "Francy, that song must have thirty verses."

"Thirty-two," Francy corrected with a giggle.

"You begin," said her mother.

"'Twas in the merry month of May
  When all the buds were swelling . . ."

Harmony filled the sunny little room as the morning breeze carried in the sweet smell of lilacs and wisteria blooming just outside. A wasp clicked against the ceiling until Francy, using the newspaper dustpan, fanned him out an open window.

"Tell me about my name," she said, interrupting the old ballad.

"Why, you're Francy Ponder. Everyone knows that."

"No, no. You know. Tell me the story of my name."

"Well, your full name," Mrs. Ponder said as she bit a thread in two, "is Wilma Francine."

Francy pushed her bare feet deep within the soft cotton and wiggled her toes. "And how'd I come by that name?"

"You tell me," her mother said, laughing. She gathered up pleats in the green linen she was sewing. "You've made me tell you often enough."

"Who named me?"

"Your big sister Elly's the one who came up with it. It was two days before you were born. Elly said, 'If it's a girl, we should call her Wilma Francine.'"

Francy waited. "But why?" she prompted.

"Well, Elly said, 'Wilma will stand for her mama and papa: Will and Mae. Francine comes from her grandmothers' names: Frances and Maxine.' And it fit together so nicely, that's just what we named you."

Francy smiled thinking about Elly, nearly grown, naming her little half sister. "But you don't ever call me that."

"Well, when you were just a tiny thing, Wilma Francine sounded too big. And when your other sister, Cora, saw you for the first time, you were dressed in a tiny white gown with pink rosebud embroidery. And you had on a tiny pink lace bonnet. She said you were the fanciest little thing—more like a doll than a baby."

Francy pouted a little at having Cora, her other half sister, in the story.

"Cora said you were so fancy that Fancy's what we should call you. Your dad laughed and said, 'I was thinking of Franny, but in the spirit of things, let's call her Francy.'"

Francy's stomach sank a little thinking of her father. Will Ponder was working far away with a crew of men, building bridges and roads. She had been so much happier when there had been enough work at his sawmill for him to make a living at home.

Francy sighed and ran her fingers through her

mother's enormous box of buttons, enjoying the sound of buttons clicking against buttons. She smiled when she found a large pearl one. "Where'd this come from?" she asked.

Mrs. Ponder spoke around the pins she held in one side of her mouth. "Why, that's what your father made when he was working last year at the button factory in Buford."

"How?"

"You know how. He told us all about searching the river for mussel shells, and the machines they used to cut the buttons, polish both sides, and drill the holes." Mrs. Ponder stood and walked to the flat iron that lay heating on the little wood stove. "And that pill bottle at the bottom of the box has three freshwater pearls that he found inside the mussels. You know all this as well as I do. Why are you such a question box today?"

"I don't know. It's just a good story." Francy ran her fingers noisily through the buttons, large and small. "Where's Daddy now, exactly?"

"Exactly? Well, I can't rightly say, but God has an eye on him, same as on us. So don't you worry."

Francy was about to beg her mother to let her try winding a bobbin at the machine when the twins began to cry.

"Sounds like Jesse and Matthew are waking each other from their naps. Would you go see to them, Francy? Just give me five minutes. I can finish this up, and we can start getting supper ready."

Chapter 2

Francy scooped up the twins and took them out to the front porch. It was the perfect ending to an early summer day, she thought. The sun was low, and a cool breeze from the river pushed up the hill. Francy sighed happily as she churned Belle's cream into butter.

The huge porch was filled with activity. Peter was swinging the twin babies in the porch swing; Eunice was shelling peas; their mother mended socks while rocking in her rocker. The sunset was fingerpainting the colors of watermelon, lemon, and strawberry across the western sky. Spring frogs sang along Briar Creek, and the whippoorwills called to each other in the woods beyond the pasture. Best of all, there was singing.

"Life's evening sun . . ." Peter sang the low bass in their father's place.

"Is sinking low . . ." Mrs. Ponder's sweet soprano joined in.

"A few more days . . ." sang the rest of the Ponders on a note somewhere in between, "and we must go. To face the deeds that we have done, where there will be no setting sun."

Out of the growing twilight a frightened voice shouted, "Mae, fasten up the dogs. It's me and the girls."

Francy groaned softly, "Oh, no." It was her half sister Cora and Cora's three daughters.

The dogs, who had been dozing on the porch, set up a racket, alerting the family that intruders were near.

"Guess Cora never heard 'Let sleeping dogs lie,'" laughed Eunice, carrying the pan filled with peas in to the kitchen.

"Peter, Chester, tie the dogs," instructed their mother, putting away her sewing. "Francy, watch the twins. Pauline, go down to the gate and help Cora with the girls."

Poor Pauline, thought Francy. *She always gets stuck helping with the girls.*

Cora entered the gate crying. "Mae, I just can't stand Jake being gone all the time."

"Yes, I know," said Mrs. Ponder in a soothing voice, her arm already around Cora's shoulder. "But be thankful your husband has a steady job conducting on the railroad. So many good men are begging for jobs."

"But I can't sleep," Cora fretted. "There were dreadful noises last night. I was sure someone was on the porch. My head's been throbbing for days, and no sleep, and the girls, and worrying about every sound . . ." Cora paused for breath as Mrs. Ponder eased her into the cedar rocking chair that Mr. Ponder had made.

"Well, you're safe now. And I'm fixing to brew you some mint tea with plenty of dill for that headache."

And so the perfect evening turned into one filled with Cora's complaints and the girls' whining. Francy wanted to climb up her favorite mulberry tree and disappear until the visitors had left. But it soon became clear that Cora was going to spend the night—and maybe several more.

Their mother offered her usual warm hospitality. And when swarms of lightning bugs began twinkling under the elm trees, she found four glass jars with lids that Peter pierced with his knife for air holes.

Cora's three daughters—Marjorie, Maude, and Miriam—all stamped and howled until they got their own jars. So Francy and Pauline shared the last one. Naturally, the shared jar filled more quickly, but the visitors squealed and pouted. "That's not fair. They're cheating. Francy's better than we are, and she's cheating to help Pauline."

Francy ached to scream at Marjorie and Maude, who were old enough to know better. But instead she said, "It isn't a contest. It's only for fun. Doesn't matter whose jar has the most. I'll put some in everyone's."

But that didn't stop Marjorie, who was only three months younger than Francy, from fussing and fuming. She ran after Francy trying to catch the same glimmering insects when the yard was a meteor shower of glowing bugs. "Be gentle," Francy warned. "You're squeezing them too hard. You'll hurt them if you're not careful."

"Be careful or you'll hurt them," mimicked Marjorie in her sourest voice. "They're just bugs, Francy Ponder. Who cares? They don't know anything."

Francy was dangerously close to losing her temper. She felt her hands tighten into fists. For a moment she couldn't speak. Very slowly she explained, "They're living creatures. We only catch them for fun and then set them free again."

"Maybe you set them free but we're keeping ours! Forever!"

"Well, they'll die in the jars!"

"Who cares? They're only stupid bugs."

"How would you like to be kept in a jar till you couldn't breathe, or be squeezed so tight that your insides smoosh out?"

"I'll smoosh all of mine if I feel like it," taunted Marjorie, "and you can't stop me, you *bug lover*."

Maude and Miriam joined their sister, echoing the jeer as they ran around the yard, laughing and shrieking, "*Bug lover, bug lover, bug lover . . .*"

"Francy," Cora complained from the porch, "why must you always make my girls take on so? That shouting is hammering stakes clean through my poor aching head."

Luckily, Eunice and Peter ended the disaster by announcing, "It's time to be getting ready for bed." So off the younger children went to wash up and to put on their pajamas.

Chapter 3

Sleep was no comfort for Francy that night. She shared her bed with Cora's girls, who complained even in their sleep, and tossed and kicked like mules.

Francy escaped early the next morning, leaving the houseguests sleeping, while she set the table and helped to dress the twins. Eunice made the biscuits and their mother fried potatoes and made gravy. Breakfast was fit for company.

"Where's Cora?" Francy asked, noticing her absence.

"She's had a real bad night, but she'll be down for breakfast," explained Mrs. Ponder.

"Too bad she doesn't ever bring anything with her but four more mouths to feed and a pain so bad she can't get out of a rocker," Francy whispered to Pauline.

Her sister smiled. "But you better not let Ma hear that kind of talk," she warned.

The troublesome trio slept through breakfast.

Afterward Francy picked strawberries—glad for a chance to be alone, even though she usually dreaded the boring chore. Next she gathered and washed spring lettuce and green onions for lunch.

The visitors, sulky and starved, appeared at midday. Their long hair was unbrushed and tangled. They wore dresses that Mrs. Ponder had made for them to wear on Sundays—much too good for playing or doing chores. And they wore shoes and socks even though it was June.

"Why didn't you wake us for breakfast?" pouted Maude.

Francy, Pauline, Eunice, and their mother soon had a savory meal on the long table. The girls all snitched biscuits before the blessing was finished and ate greedily as dishes were passed.

The salad of spring lettuce, green onions, and crispy bits of bacon tasted wonderful. Eunice's biscuits were light and delicious. The pots of greens were enough for an army, and the family enjoyed the garden's first peas and creamed new potatoes. For dessert there were the berries Francy had picked, layered between a shortcake rich with Belle's sweet butter and topped with rich cream.

Everyone ate heartily. Marjorie, however, ate as if the world was ending immediately after the meal. Helping after helping of salad, biscuits, beans, and greens disappeared from her plate.

"How can someone as scrawny as a scarecrow hold so much?" Pauline whispered. "She's eatin' more than Peter."

Finally Marjorie announced, "I'm stuffed. But it's all so good I never want to stop eating. Mama, why can't you ever fix meals like this? Gran'Mae is a much better cook than you. I don't know why you can't get her to teach you something."

Heavy silence fell over the room. Francy stared at her plate. She was too embarrassed to look at Cora or her mother. Without doubt, her mother was the best cook in the county and Cora one of the worst, but Francy couldn't believe that anyone—even Marjorie—would criticize her own mother, especially in front of family.

The silence went on for what felt like hours. At last Mrs. Ponder spoke. "It's time for the shortcake. Eunice, you and Francy please clear the table. Chester, go fetch the cream from the springhouse. And Pauline, would you please whip it? Peter, please watch the twins, and I'll get bowls and clean spoons."

As everyone scurried in different directions, Mrs. Ponder spoke matter-of-factly. "Marjorie, our meals seem special because you've come visiting. But the truth is that I don't make the meals."

"Of course you do. I see you cooking all the time."

"I have lots of help, just like when I work at Mrs. Trundle's. And it takes us all to make good meals. If you help your mama, you'll learn to be a great cook, too."

Marjorie just snorted in response.

The shortcake was the best of the season. Everyone was full and lazy—content to sit an extra moment at the table and talk.

Suddenly Marjorie let out a scream.

"What on earth!" said Cora.

Marjorie screamed again and again, pushing her chair away from the table, doubled over in pain.

The twins in their high chairs started to cry.

"Ohhh," Marjorie yelled, "ohhh, my stomach. Mama, I've got to go!"

"Well, land's sake, go! Don't just sit and holler. Take off for the outhouse!" said Cora.

"I can't, Mama—there is a whole mess of wasps in there."

The twins cried louder.

"Just shoo 'em out," said Mrs. Ponder.

"No! Ohhh, I've got to go NOW! Mama, you have to come and kill the wasps. You know how scared they make me."

The twins sobbed as the conversation became more frantic.

Cora looked panicky. She was more terrified of insects than all three of her daughters put together. "Francy," Cora pleaded, "please walk Marjorie to the outhouse. You're not afraid of anything. You're as brave as your mama."

Francy was about to protest when her mother shot her a glance that said "Please go."

Marjorie cried and moaned all the way down the winding path. "I don't see why you have an old outhouse anyway. It's disgusting."

Their toilet was brand new, built of lumber from Will Ponder's mill. Francy thought of reminding Marjorie that her family had had indoor plumbing a little less than a year. Most of the homes around still had a backyard privy. But what was the use?

Finally the girls arrived at the outhouse. Francy looked over the inside while Marjorie screamed and cried for her to hurry.

"All clear," she shouted as Marjorie ran past her and slammed the door.

"Keep talking so I know you're still there," demanded her cousin between groans.

"You shouldn't eat so many greens all at once," suggested Francy, impatient at having to treat Marjorie as if she were the twins' age. She leaned on the building and let the warm sun bake her bare arms. Then she flicked a mosquito and her fingernail accidentally scraped the oak planks.

"What's that?" called Marjorie from inside.

"Just a wasp," lied the guard. "I'll keep 'em off."

"Are there many?"

"Several," said Francy with a grin. "Maybe a dozen. But there's only a couple of knotholes and I'm guarding them."

"Don't you let any of 'em in!" screamed Marjorie. "Don't you dare let *any* of those nasty things in here."

"I'll do my best," Francy promised before covering her mouth to keep from giggling.

She flicked the walls every so often, holding her mouth tightly closed.

"What's that?" the captive screamed.

Instead of answering Francy flicked the wall.

"Francy?"

Click.

"Francy, are you there? Francy, for heaven's sake answer me . . ."

Click, click, click.

"FRANCY," Marjorie screamed. "FRANCY, WHERE ARE YOU?"

"I'm here," panted Francy. "It's all right. I got most of 'em. I had to leave one knothole unguarded a minute while I chased 'em. Did any get in?"

"IN?" shrieked Marjorie. "It's dark in here. How should I know?"

"Do you hear anything?"

Click, click, click.

"Oh, Francy, there's one in here. Help me."

"The door's locked. Don't panic."

"Francy, I'm locked in a stinky old outhouse with a swarm of wasps! How can I not panic?"

"Say, Marjorie, did you ever wonder whether bugs can talk to one another?"

"Are you crazy?"

Francy was doubled over trying not to laugh out loud.

"Not like people talk. But, you know, somehow maybe they communicate."

"What are you raving about?"

"Didn't you ever wonder if a cricket could tell an ant a secret? Or if an earthworm could warn mayflies to stay away from fishermen?"

"Francy, just guard the knotholes till I finish."

"I just thought maybe . . . well, maybe, lightning bugs might be able to tell wasps somehow . . . maybe

17

by flashing code or something." Francy kept her voice perfectly honest. "Maybe they could tell bees and hornets and yellow jackets and wasps about people who think bugs are meant to be smothered in jars . . ."

"Francy Ponder, you wicked beast! You're not guarding me. And I'm going to tell on you the second I get out of here!" screamed Marjorie. "The very second!"

"I know you will," Francy said, bursting into giggles. She had held them back so long they had given her hiccups.

Chapter 4

Things moved along at their regular pace—until Francy's mother got sick.

Cora had stopped by one afternoon and found Mrs. Ponder slumped over her sewing machine. She sent Peter running all the way to town to get the doctor. Cora's husband, Jake, on leave from his conducting job, gave Peter and Doc Woerther a lift home in his shiny Model A.

"Maude and Miriam, you be good girls for your daddy," said Cora, unloading a basket of supplies. "Marjorie, you're old enough to stay here with me and help out."

"Tick fever," Doc Woerther whispered to Cora.

"How bad?"

"Very," he said, shaking his head. "We won't know for several days."

Jake returned the next morning and took Peter with him to help track down the road crew where Will Ponder was working.

Mrs. Trundle came from the boarding house as soon as news spread. "Eunice, take this block of ice," the old woman commanded, "and you girls keep your ma bathed in icy cold water day and night. Cover the block with sawdust and keep it in the springhouse, and it'll last even in this heat. When you're near to runnin' out, send word and I'll come with more."

"Thank you," Eunice said.

"Not necessary. Mae'd do the same for me. Best friend a body could have. And the best cook I ever hired." The stern old innkeeper choked back tears. Then, her voice firm again, she said, "Remember the compresses. And send word when you need more."

Cora, who usually considered herself too good to fry an egg, rose to the occasion and helped cook meals, mind the twins, and nurse Mae. She cried a lot, which frightened Francy more than the worried look Doc Woerther wore on his daily visits.

"We must be brave," Francy told the twins over and over. "Daddy will be home soon, and then everything will be all right."

Meals were cooked as usual, but the food seemed to stick in their throats. Cora insisted that Marjorie help out, which made more work for the others. She tried to help Chester in the garden, but she accidentally hoed down a tomato plant heavy with green tomatoes. When Pauline took her berry picking, she was so terrified of the bees that she ran back home with blue fingers and a briar-torn dress.

Jelly making was simple, though, and Marjorie

seemed to enjoy learning as Eunice patiently explained what to do. Marjorie tested the sweet-smelling nectar by dipping the spoon into the boiling liquid and holding it up to see if the drops rolled together quickly or jelled to form two separate droplets. Scrubbing the jelly jars also went smoothly. But while they were melting paraffin to seal the jars, the small pan on the back of the stove caught fire. Thus Marjorie's jelly making ended.

"Come with me," Francy offered. "You can help me bring in Belle and watch me milk her. You've worked enough for one day."

Marjorie carried Cynthia, her favorite doll, as the two girls wandered through the pasture listening for the gentle tinkle of Belle's cowbell. They found a turtle, which Marjorie was afraid to touch but stubbornly claimed as hers saying, "I saw it first, Francy. But you have to carry it for me, 'cause I've got Cynthia."

The sound of the clinking cowbell led them through the pasture to the edge of the woods where Belle was grazing.

Francy drove Belle home, tying her in the stall. Then she scoured the shiny milking bucket. Soon sprays of milk danced in the pail. Marjorie played with the turtle, turning it over with a stick whenever it wandered too far away.

"Let me try milking," Marjorie pleaded after becoming bored with the turtle.

Common sense said no. "Not today," said Francy. "Maybe in the morning."

But Marjorie begged and begged.

"Fine," Francy sighed at last. "Sit like me and put your cheek against her side. Talk to her in a real soft voice."

Marjorie sat on the stool and leaned her cheek against Belle's side. "Nice cow," she cooed. "Nice old Belle."

"That's it. You're doing fine," said Francy. The gentle cow screwed her head around to watch the stranger.

"Squeeze and pull. Squeeze and pull," Francy encouraged. The milk came slowly and with great effort, but it seemed Marjorie had finally found a job she could do.

Then it happened.

A horsefly zoomed right past Marjorie's ear. She gave an ear-piercing scream, leaped from the stool, and overturned the bucket.

Frightened, Belle let out a low, bawling moo.

Francy scrambled to save a portion of the milk as Marjorie, still screaming at the top of her lungs, ran out past the honking geese in the yard.

Carefully, Francy cleaned the bucket and tried to finish milking Belle, but the cow was too tense. Francy would have to start over in the morning.

As Francy put everything in its proper place, she wondered if Marjorie would ever be able to complete a job. When Francy finished up, she went back to the house to sit with her mother.

Cora came out of the sickroom crying. She grabbed Francy in the only hug the girl could ever remember from her half sister. After a long time, Cora managed to say, "Poor, poor child. Poor little thing."

Francy was uncomfortable and tried to pull away. Cora kept hugging and crying. "I was just your age when my ma . . ."

Francy broke free and ran into her mother's darkened room. Eunice was bathing her in ice water. "How is she?" cried Francy. "Is Mama all right?"

"No better," said Eunice slowly. "But no worse. Doc Woerther thinks there will be a change soon."

Mrs. Ponder moaned in her sleep. Francy leaned over and kissed her mother's feverish cheek before disappearing into the sewing room. The others could worry over supper. She sat at the old sewing machine and prayed until dawn.

Chapter 5

"What's that?" questioned Marjorie.

"An ax handle," Francy said.

"What for?"

"I'm going to gather the eggs."

"With an ax handle?"

"No." Francy was impatient at having to explain. "There are two roosters in with the hens and they're meaner than the devil himself. I use this ax handle to keep them away."

"But Ma's saying all the time how you're not afraid of anything."

Francy felt herself blushing. "Look, Marjorie, I've got to get the eggs. You can come along or stay here."

"If they're so mean, why don't you get rid of them?"

"Well . . ." she stammered, "they're kind of Daddy's pets. He always says how he loves to hear 'em crowing in the morning. And they're good as gold when he's around."

The girls made their way to the henhouse with water buckets and feed. Marjorie held the ax handle while Francy opened the gate and carried in the buckets.

"You wait here."

"No!" Marjorie protested. "I'm not afraid."

"Suit yourself."

The girls filled feed troughs and cleaned and refilled watering jars. They inspected a clucking hen with a brood of fuzzy chicks, but all the while they kept an eye on the two roosters circling the pen. Marjorie, standing guard at the door during the egg gathering, was nearly knocked over when Francy ran out suddenly.

"What's wrong?" Marjorie asked, ax handle raised and ready to strike.

"Need the hoe."

Marjorie shrieked as she saw Francy carrying out a snake draped over the hoe. Its slender body was lumpy with the broken eggs it had swallowed whole.

Francy got rid of the snake before she finished the egg gathering. Emerging from the gloomy henhouse, she was blinded for a moment by the July sun. When her eyes focused, there stood Marjorie, pale and silent.

"What's the matter? The snake won't . . ."

"I never meant to," Marjorie stammered. "It was an accident . . . he came at me from behind and I . . . I . . . I killed him." She pointed.

Francy laughed out loud. There on the ground was one of the roosters that had plagued her for so long.

"Why are you laughing? Won't your daddy be mad?"

"I think he'll get over it," said Francy, still smiling. "Have you ever plucked a chicken?"

"Of course not!"

"Well, boil some water 'cause you're fixing to learn." Then, skipping carefully so as not to crack the eggs, Francy sang, "And we'll all have chicken and dumplings when she comes, when she comes. Yes, we'll all have chicken and dumplings when she comes."

Both girls laughed and sang as they returned to the house to start dinner.

Chapter 6

Even though there were no fireworks, it was the best Fourth of July in Francy's memory. Her mother opened her eyes, smiled, and sipped broth. Doc Woerther laughed for the first time since Mrs. Ponder got the fever. Mrs. Trundle brought more ice, as well as fresh cinnamon rolls. Jake was coming home with Peter to help celebrate.

The family had just begun to pass steaming bowls of dumplings late that afternoon. They didn't hear the Model A crunching along the gravel road, or the men slipping quietly through the back door.

"Looks like you folks eat mighty high off the hog when I'm away," Mr. Ponder said, laughing.

"We brought you a surprise," said Peter.

"Daddy!" Will Ponder's children screamed, running to surround him with bear hugs. Jake quickly made his excuses and took Cora and Marjorie to see the fireworks at the river. Mr.

Ponder stood looking joyfully at his family.

"You all go on ahead and enjoy this meal. We'll get reacquainted in a spell." He kissed them all once more and disappeared into his wife's room, remaining until well after the whippoorwills had begun their twilight serenade.

For the first time in months, the Ponders were all together. The cozy house embraced them as they rested through the warm night.

Chapter 7

Every pitcher in the house was filled with fragrant honeysuckle. Francy had made sure the room smelled as good as an evening's breeze.

Her mother sat on the edge of the bed brushing her long hair before pinning it into a topknot. She hummed as she combed, pausing at times as if the combing took all her strength.

"Francy," her mother said slowly, "you needn't keep fussing over me. I'm fine. Weak, but fine."

"It's no trouble," Francy said, as she arranged the fragrant blossoms in the blue-and-white pitcher on the nightstand.

"I'm mighty proud of how my children pulled together during my illness. But everyone says how you outworked them all." Mae examined her hair in the dresser mirror, patting a few strays into place. "You're a mighty brave girl and you know how much we depend on you, but now I want you to stop worrying over me."

"I wasn't worried," Francy said with a smile. "I just couldn't stand Cora crying all the time. That would put anyone on pins and needles. But I knew from the first that you'd be fine." Francy hugged her mother gently, careful not to hurt her.

This is the best feeling of all, thought Francy. *Mama's all right.*

Chapter 8

Mr. Ponder was gone most mornings since his homecoming, scouring the county for jobs. He had visited every maker of ax handles, barrel staves, fencing, and rough lumber—with no success.

"This is the hottest day I can remember," Pauline complained, as she and Francy hoed long rows of tomatoes.

"Well, July is supposed to be hot," Francy answered, picking a large green worm off the underside of a leaf and crushing it with the hoe. "Did you bring any rag strips? This plant needs to be tied up higher on the stake."

"I forgot," answered Pauline. "But I'm so hot I'd gladly tear my dress into strips."

"Maybe Mama will let us take the little ones to the creek after lunch. We haven't waded since before she took sick."

"Don't count on it," Pauline said, wiping her

face on her apron. "We still have all these to pick."

"Pau-ween! Fran-cee!" called the twins from the backyard.

"Saved by the twins." Pauline smiled. "Who's the lucky one who gets to trade a hoe for watching that pair of chipmunks?"

"You can," offered Francy. "If they can't take your mind off this heat, nothing can. I'll finish out the row."

The mouthwatering smells of fried squash and simmering sweet corn greeted Francy when she finally trudged up the hill from the garden. Eunice was fixing lunch. Pauline was nowhere in sight, but Francy laughed at Jesse and Matthew running the length of the great stone porch.

Suddenly they stopped playing and jabbered something that Francy couldn't understand. Then they toddled slowly to the high end of the porch and stood smiling with their arms stretched out as far as they could reach.

Pauline returned from the kitchen, where she'd just set the table. "What are you young sprouts up to now?"

The boys didn't speak. They just smiled at Pauline and Francy and stretched out their arms even farther.

"Come on, what are you playing?"

Finally Jesse said, "Hug." Their smiles were identical.

"Hug what?" asked Pauline.

"Hug it!" said the twins.

Pauline stretched out her arms. Sure enough, a cool breeze embraced her. As Francy walked up, Pauline exclaimed, "They're hugging the wind! Feel it, Francy? The twins are hugging a wonderful, cool breeze."

For a moment they all stood high on the porch, their arms reaching out to the cooling breeze. Within minutes the wind grew stronger, bringing clouds that blocked the scorching sun. "Thank goodness," their mother said, putting the last of the steaming dishes on the noonday table. "The garden might get watered without us lugging buckets from the creek."

Everyone was laughing as they washed up on the back porch. The cool air refreshed their spirits. They were about to sit down to lunch when suddenly Mrs. Ponder called from the window. "Everyone, quick, get to the cellar! Now!"

Pauline and Francy looked at each other—a storm was coming! Each girl grabbed a twin. Eunice and their mother grabbed lamps and matches.

Peter said, "I'll go drive Belle up to the stable."

"Belle's smart enough to take care of herself. Leave everything and run."

The cellar smelled like the entrance to an old bat cave, but the kerosene lamps threw a warm glow on the shelves lined with hundreds of Mason jars. Two sixty-gallon barrels stood in corners—one filled with sauerkraut and the other with pickles.

The Ponders were crowded in the underground

pantry, but it was safe and quiet. The heavy doors sealed out the rolling thunder. Soon hail began pelting the six-inch-thick wooden doors that were closed above them as the storm raged.

The twins started to cry. Mrs. Ponder quickly began finger games. She chanted the words calmly, "This is father's knives and forks. This is mother's table. This is sister's looking glass. This is baby's cradle."

The older children showed Jesse and Matthew how to weave their fingers and twist their hands to play. Soon the battering hailstones died down, and the twins were content to be the center of attention. Everyone chanted the old rhymes as the babies tried to perform the actions.

The storm quieted. Impatiently, Francy urged Peter to raise the door and peek outside. Then there was one last deafening crash right over their heads.

The twins hugged each other tightly. All was quiet. After a few minutes, their mother stood up and listened. "Peter, I believe it's passed. Take a look outside."

Peter climbed two of the five stairs and pushed against the slanting doors. Then he pushed harder, grunting with all his might. He looked back at his mother. "It won't budge."

"Chet, help your brother," said Mrs. Ponder.

Chester was only twelve, but nearly as tall as Peter. Standing on the stairway, the boys strained and pushed against the slanting doors for several minutes, but to no avail. Then Eunice and Pauline joined their brothers on the stairway, trying to force the doors open.

"Sit a spell," said their mother.

Minutes passed. Hours passed. Francy thought perhaps days might be slipping by.

"Dim the lamp, Eunice," said their mother softly as she turned the other lamp completely out.

Everyone stared at her. "It's a bit too bright on my eyes," she explained. "Let's sing."

Harmony filled the cellar. Afterward everyone was hoarse from singing. Peter found some twine in his pocket and cut strips with his knife so Eunice could teach everyone how to play cat's cradle, saucer and teacup, and, best of all, Jacob's ladder.

Francy was starving. She couldn't help thinking about the uneaten meal they had hastily abandoned. The cranky twins huddled together for a nap.

Everyone had grown tired and stiff from their cramped positions when the ringing sound of an ax striking wood startled them. The boys shouted loudly to let their rescuer know they were trapped below.

"Hush," their mother said, as Jesse and Matthew fussed at being wakened.

Only traces of what must have been a beautiful sunset hung in the western sky when Mr. Ponder finally opened the cellar doors. The captives climbed out, stretching their backs and smelling the cool air. They all marveled at the giant hickory that the lightning had toppled over the cellar doors.

Kerosene lamps revealed the noon meal—cold and withered—still resting on the table. But within minutes Mrs. Ponder had a warm supper ready for her hungry family.

Talk came from all sides at once as the children told their father about the terrible storm and being stuck in the cellar.

Mr. Ponder patiently listened before telling his own news. He had been trapped in Wainwright's feed store to wait out the storm, where he had passed the time with Lester Odom, a childhood friend. After a long talk, Mr. Ponder had convinced Odom, a river guide, that he needed a larger boat. And who better to build it? So Mr. Ponder had a job—a job that would pay cash!

Chapter 9

The whole family had taken turns picking, raking, and hoeing in the garden. The summer had grown very dry, and buckets of water had to be carried from the creek to the wilting plants. It was 614 steps—Francy had counted. The well was much closer, but they couldn't chance letting it run dry.

Today Francy hummed gently as she cut the okra, filling a small basket with tender pods. She tried hard to resist the urge to wipe her sweaty face. She knew this would spread the plant's prickly fuzz and start unbearable itching. Pauline sat in the shade of the elms, shelling peas and watching the twins. Their mother and Eunice were taking naps before starting the noon meal. They had canned string beans most of the night. "Night's the best time," their mother always said. "Keeps the heat of the stove from cooking the cooks."

Their father shouted from where he was working

in the garden. "Peter, you feel up to racing a bee?"

"I'm ready," Peter answered from the other end of the garden.

Father and son watched a bee gather nectar from a cucumber blossom. When the insect had a full load, it zoomed off with Peter and his father running in pursuit. It was the third time this week they had tried to find the tree where the bee's hive was.

Francy watched them run toward the woods. "Think they want the honey or just want to get away from this garden?" she said, laughing.

"Probably both," answered Pauline.

"Dinner," Eunice called from the house. Francy and the others hurried up the hill. They washed their hands in a tin basin on the back porch, carefully saving every drop of water in a bucket. Later they would carry it to the garden when the sun was setting. That way the water would have a chance to soak into the parched ground.

After the meal, Francy watched Jesse and Matthew while Pauline cleaned jelly jars for the blackberry jam their mother was making. Chester, buckets in hand, went to search for more berries.

At midafternoon, Peter returned. Without any explanation, he grabbed an ax and a metal tub, then ran back to the woods. It was early evening when he and their father arrived home. Between them they carried the tub, which was almost overflowing with honey.

"Will Ponder, did you leave the bees anything to

winter on?" his wife said, looking at the enormous tub.

"Plenty," he answered. "The white oak they're in has a hollow nearly as big as that boat we're building."

The children licked sticky fingers and chewed on honeycomb gum as their mother sealed jar after jar of honey—some strained clear, some with comb showing through the jar.

"I need all hands," said Mrs. Ponder, "to carry the honey to the cellar. We can also take jelly jars that are cool enough."

In the welcome cool of the cellar, the youngsters never tired of marveling over the endless bounty stored in Mason jars. They delighted in peeking at the jams, pickles, peaches, beans, beets, and berries. They thought of the cobblers and stews they would feast on when snow covered the garden and ice turned the Ozark hills into a glistening fairyland.

"Tonight we'll have breakfast for supper," Mrs. Ponder announced.

Everyone cheered.

Besides eggs and fried potatoes, there were feathery-light pancakes, steaming hot to melt dollops of Belle's sweet butter and smothered with all the honey the children could ask for.

Chapter 10

"You shouldn't feel that way, Francy," said her father, dipping the wide brush and smoothing the green paint up and down the prow of the boat.

"Well, Mama was counting on the sale of this boat," Francy complained at the mill. "And she doesn't need to be getting sick again . . ."

"No, she doesn't. But never blame hard times on good neighbors." The outside of the boat was getting its third coat of dark green paint. "It's not Lester Odom's fault that the men from the city can't afford fishing trips this year."

"I hate him anyway!" Francy said. She stared at her bare feet. "Gettin' everyone's hopes up."

Francy's father looked at her sternly. "I know you're worried about your mama. But I don't ever want to hear that kind of talk again, Francy Ponder! Especially against someone who saved your people from worse times than these."

"Worse times?" asked Francy.

"No matter how bad things get, Francy, just remember someone's always been through worse." Mr. Ponder lit the lantern and continued painting in the evening's dying light. "Lester and I grew up on neighboring farms. Played together as boys. Lester is as good a man as you'll ever find. Now hand me that turpentine can."

The crickets singing in the trees just below the mill were the only sound. Francy dangled her feet and pouted in silence.

"I was a shade older than you, Francy. It was February, and my little sisters were spread out on the floor making Valentines for school. Pa was off hunting. Ma was sitting in her rocker counting egg money."

Francy stayed silent, acting as if she weren't paying attention.

"I remember it was dark even before supper. Ma had lit a lamp so we could see, but the hook pulled loose from the wall. The lamp hit the floor, and the fire spread fast! Ma screamed and grabbed the baby, and we all ran outside."

Francy stopped swinging her feet and stared at her father, who never paused from his painting.

"We lost everything in that fire. Dead of winter . . . no house, no coats, no money."

"Why haven't you ever told us this story?" Francy questioned from her perch on the tool rack.

"Lester Odom's folks saw the flames. They were the first ones there. They took us in . . . all winter

. . . till we could rebuild. They had a big family and it was crowded." Mr. Ponder moved the light back and forth along the boat, checking for any spots he had missed.

"Others gave quilts and clothes and what they could. But the Odoms! Well, they went the extra mile. After a night or two, they could have packed us off. But they didn't. And they never let on that they were doing anything special."

The stars shone now, and it was totally dark except for the lantern. Francy thought about her family, their sturdy rock house, and what it must be like not to have a home.

Mr. Ponder soaked his brush in turpentine and hammered the lid tight on the paint can. Then he proudly inspected his paint job. The wet paint glistened under the lantern.

"Let's go home, little lady," he said, swinging Francy down by his side. The two of them slowly climbed up the hill and listened to the singing coming from the front porch.

"Those were worse times, Francy," her father said, putting his arm around her shoulder. "Not for everyone. But worse for our family."

Chapter 11

The cool air smelled like fresh water long before they could see the river through the trees. The family glowed with excitement as they all helped carry the boat down the steep bank.

The long craft floated in the shallows, chained to the root of a sycamore tree. Everyone loaded picnic baskets, quilts, and jugs into the boat's bottom.

"Stand back from that bank. The water's swift," Mrs. Ponder nervously reminded the children.

The morning mist had not yet burned off the stream. The eery cawing of unseen crows carried for miles on the water. With gear stowed, the family boarded to occupy the six double seats. The twins were well attended to, and Peter and his father manned the oars at each end of the boat.

The boat glided silently upstream in the calm water, away from the channel's mighty current. The oars scarcely disturbed the silent mist rising from the tranquil surface. Mr. Ponder pointed out herons standing on one leg, caves opening into the limestone cliffs, and ancient red cedars.

As the sun grew stronger, scores of turtles, ranging in size from buttons to barrels, could be seen sunning themselves atop logs. An hour after the launch their father asked, "Who's ready for fishing?"

Everyone clamored for bait and poles. Even the twins fished with help from the older children. Soon they had caught a good number.

By noon Francy exclaimed, "It seems as if we've been on the water all day."

"Ready to quit already?" her father asked.

They landed on a gravel bar where the younger children could swim without the danger of the strong current. Chester and Peter built a fire, and their mother soon had fish frying along with potatoes and hush puppies, a delicious cornmeal treat.

The mouthwatering smell was the only thing that could coax the hungry swimmers out of the crystal water. Gallons of lemonade washed down the fish. To top it off, they feasted on pies that their mother and Eunice had made.

After lunch, all the Ponders, large and small, frolicked like otters in the water. Even Mrs. Ponder waded into the cool water.

"Sold or not, this is a fine boat," laughed their father.

They rowed farther up the river to a place where

there was a shady apron of sand and gravel on which the twins could take a nap on an old quilt. The others could fish, swim, collect mussel shells and pretty nuggets of gravel, or swing from a rope to drop into a pool of blue-green water.

"Francy, I declare," said her mother as the girl came out of the water, "you've grown a whole crop of freckles in just one day."

"She's as speckled as a tiger lily," Pauline laughed.

Francy made a face at her.

"Don't pay any mind," Mrs. Ponder said. "Freckles are beautiful and a sign of intelligence, to boot."

Francy smiled, not minding in the least if she became as spotted as a guinea hen if it meant having this much fun.

The twins woke from their nap, and Francy danced with them in the shallow water. "Giddee up, horsey, go to town; Oh, little horsey, don't fall down!" She would dunk them up to their chins, and they would emerge giggling and shouting, "Again! Again, again!"

As the afternoon turned to dusk, Mr. Ponder headed the boat toward home, letting the current do the work. He steered the long craft around reeds and rocks with only an occasional touch of his paddle. They ate cold biscuits spread with wild honey as they slid silently past deer drinking peacefully along the shore.

"Just listen to the night sounds," their mother

said. The silence changed to the croaking of bullfrogs and the singing of crickets in the trees along the banks. Night birds began their sad singing, and the exhausted children rode in wonder, soothed by the murmur of the stream swirling around fallen trees and boulders.

Their hair and clothes dried, but their skin felt cool long after they arrived back at the big rock house.

"Daddy," Francy asked, "since Lester Odom can't afford it, can we keep the boat forever?"

"Maybe we'll do just that. Least ways for right now." He kissed her freckled forehead before she darted off to bed.

"Don't forget your prayers," said her mother, still unpacking picnic kettles and jars.

"I won't," answered Francy, running back to give her mother an extra squeeze. "I won't. I love you."

Chapter 12

It was a Thursday in late August when Cora and the girls came to get Belle. Mrs. Ponder was up in the sewing room sprucing up old draperies. The older boys were cutting wood down at the sawmill. In the kitchen, Francy and Pauline were slicing apples to dry in the sun.

"Francy," her father called from the garden.

"Mind the twins," she told Pauline, before hurrying to the garden.

"Francy, go drive Belle up to the stable."

"It's way too early to milk!"

"Do as I say," her father said in a tone that meant no more questions.

Belle was far out in the pasture lying in the shade of the trees, contentedly chewing her cud. The gentle Jersey had no intention of wandering about in the heat of an August afternoon.

Francy had to work harder than ever to drive

Belle up the hill to her stable. "Come on, Belle!" she pleaded, waving a stick and urging Belle to her feet. Grasshoppers flew up from the dry grass as she yelled and ran, circling the cow.

"Get going, Belle!" Belle's cowbell gently clanked as the animal finally started to climb to the stable. "Don't you go trying to circle back!" Francy warned. "Come on, Belle!"

Francy and Belle were both hot and confused when they finally reached the stable. Her father was waiting there with Belle's halter rope. "Good-bye, old girl," he said, patting the cow's neck as he took off the huge bell and slid on the rope halter. "You've been a good friend to us." He patted the cow, who stood patiently swishing flies with her tail. "Be good to your new family, girl."

"New family?" Francy exclaimed, staring wide-eyed at her father.

He did not speak, but simply led Belle slowly to the house, where Cora and the three girls were waiting. "Here she is, Cora. She'll give good milk all through the winter."

"I hope so. These three keep me cleaned out most of the time." Cora fanned herself with last week's paper. "My, it's hot." She pushed back her bonnet and wiped her face with a handkerchief. She stared at Belle but made no attempt to get up. "Where's Mae?"

"She's finishing some sewing for Mrs. Douglas," Will said, not mentioning she was finishing it upstairs and not at the Douglas house.

"Surprised anyone can afford sewing these days," Cora said, fanning away with the newspaper. "Well, we'll just trouble you for some water and then we'll be on our way." Cora watched Belle chew her cud. "'Course, it's mighty hot to drive a cow. We could stay a spell and let you all have this evening's milk," she offered.

"Best you take her quick so everyone can get used to the change," Mr. Ponder said. "Francy, bring some water from the springhouse so's everyone can have a cool drink."

Francy moved toward the springhouse as if someone else had taken over her body. She had heard the words, but her mind refused to believe what she'd heard. Belle was family. They could no more let Cora take her than take Jesse or Matthew. Inside the cool springhouse Francy cried. But only for a minute.

"Hurry, Francy," she heard her father's voice calling. She splashed cold water over her red eyes and wiped her face on the hem of her dress.

Plunking the water bucket and dipper on the porch, she disappeared before Marjorie and Maude could torment her about Belle. Upstairs, Francy found her mother with eyes as red as her own. "They're stealing Belle!" Francy sobbed. "Cora and those . . . those girls are stealing Belle!"

"Not stealing," her mother corrected softly. "Buying. They need a cow and we need money. If not them, we'd have to sell her to someone else. At least we know she'll be taken care of."

"Why?" Francy asked, tears starting to flow again. "Why? Belle is . . ." The lump in her throat cut off her words.

"Hard times," her mother answered with a voice Francy knew she was working to keep steady. After a few minutes she went on. "We have bills past due, taxes, and little worth selling."

Francy climbed on the bale of cotton in the corner, turning her face to the wall so her mother couldn't see the hot tears streaming down her face.

"Belle's a good cow. Raised her from a calf. Hate to see her go. Twins still need milk." Her mother paused as if out of breath. "And the cottage cheese and butter bought us a little coffee and sugar at the general store." Mae stopped her work and rubbed her eyes. "But we'll live without coffee and we've got honey for sweetening."

Francy tried hard not to cry out loud. But the harder she tried to hold back, the tighter the knot in her throat grew.

Her mother spoke softly. "Belle's in for a visit anytime we get to town. And remember how you hated churning? That's one less thing for you to do."

A long time passed without a word. The voices of Cora and the girls making their good-byes drifted up through the open windows. "I hate them," Francy whispered to herself, "I hate them! I hate them! I hate them!"

"Cora's your sister. Remember that."

"Half sister!" corrected Francy.

"Well, the *sister* part is more important than the *half* part. I know she gets on your nerves. Things just spill out of her mouth. She grew up without a mother to teach her. But she's family. No matter what, Cora and the girls are family."

Francy didn't look convinced.

"Besides," said her mother, "maybe Belle's a blessing to them. Maybe she'll bless Cora and the girls the way she's blessed you."

"What do you mean?"

Mae bit her thread in two with a snap. "Remember, those girls will have to learn to milk. And churn. And make cheese. And feed Belle. There'll be no pasture in town. They'll have to clean her stable and put down clean straw."

Francy sat up on the cotton and hugged her knees. The tears stopped.

"Cora doesn't know how to milk. And the girls' daddy is gone most of the time." Her mother talked softly as she wound the long bobbin with blue thread to match the drapery fabric.

Francy looked out the window as if it were a crystal ball into the future. She rested her chin on her knees and rocked back and forth on the cotton. The freckles on her nose pushed together as she thought about Cora's girls tending a cow.

"You're right," Francy said jubilantly. "They'll bring Belle back home inside a week . . . soon as they find out the milk pitcher won't fill itself."

Mae looked startled. "Pray that they *can* learn to make a go, Francy," she responded, pedaling the wrought iron treadle under the sewing machine. "If not, Belle will be sold. And we can't afford to buy her back."

Francy's pleasure vanished. "No," she cried. "Belle can't be sold! They'll just have to learn! Those screeching tomcats will learn even if I have to walk to town twice a day to teach them!"

Her mother smiled. "That's my girl."

"May I be excused the rest of the day?"

"Why?" asked Mrs. Ponder.

"I've got to catch up to Cora. I've got to go with them and show Marjorie and Maude how to wash Belle's bag . . . how to lean their cheek into her side and talk real soft while she stands for milking. Belle will be nervous enough with new people, a new stable, and no pasture. If one of those silly girls gets kicked, their daddy might decide they shouldn't keep a cow after all. But Belle will know me and that will help. Please let me go. And I'll spend the night so there's a friendly soul to milk her in the morning."

Her mother studied her a moment with a wrinkled forehead. Then she let out a long sigh. "What you say is true. Ask your father. It's fine by me if he approves."

"Thank you," Francy said, hugging her mother tightly. "Thank you for helping me see."

Cora and the girls were leading Belle up the last hill before town when Francy caught up with them.

Chapter 13

It was the third morning of school when Miss Faye finished the spelling class and said, "It's too beautiful for us to be indoors. What do you think of eating lunch under the cedars near the ball field?"

Everyone cheered including Francy. She had wished so hard to be in Miss Faye's class. Miss Faye was the nicest and prettiest teacher in the whole school.

The only fly in the ointment was Marjorie, who sat two rows over in the very front. But even that didn't seem so bad since Francy had been stopping almost every day after school to help with Belle.

Marjorie's father had praised Francy that very morning. "I really appreciate your coming by, Francy. My girls aren't natural-born milkmaids such as you." He chewed a piece of hay and rubbed Belle's favorite spot right between her horns.

"I love Belle. And I'm happy to help out," said Francy shyly.

"Well, you're a good worker. Don't know how we'd have managed without your help."

Francy had beamed with Jake's praise as she leaned against Belle's warm side.

It was when she was carrying the milk inside that she overheard Jake arguing with Cora. "I never said Marjorie was lazy. Our girls just aren't used to farm chores. But you were the one who insisted we needed a cow. Begged and badgered for days." His voice was a hard whisper. "Now you say sell Belle. Well, the world's gone bust, Cora. We'd sell her for pennies and still have to buy milk."

Cora acted even more put out when Francy mentioned that Belle's stall needed to be cleaned and the water trough filled.

"Buy a cow, pay for feed," Cora mumbled. "Then give away the milk." Francy knew the quart or so of milk Jake sent along to the Ponders was his way of thanking her.

Francy turned her thoughts away from Belle as Miss Faye led the class outside. September had the bluest sky Francy could recall. Today, from under the cedars in the school yard, it was bluer than ever. She had carefully picked a clean patch of moss as a seat so her new jumper wouldn't get stained. All morning her friends had complimented her.

"Francy, that is the prettiest thing."

"Francy Ponder, you are the luckiest girl to have a ma that sews so fine."

"That is the prettiest corduroy. Navy with those tiny yellow roses."

"And a headband to match. I just envy you."

Francy rejoiced inside but tried hard not to act too proud. "Mama said it was still too warm to wear," she admitted. "But I just couldn't wait. Mama stayed up late finishing the blouse."

Soon everyone was relaxing in the shade eating lunch. Francy sat with a group of girls not far from the tree where Miss Faye leaned. Everyone was eating and talking when Marjorie began to giggle. "Look at Francy's lunch!" she said loudly. "It still has ashes on it!"

Francy blushed, glancing down at the baked sweet potato her mother had sent. It had roasted in the dying embers of the wood stove as her mother worked on the pale yellow blouse. Suddenly Francy had no appetite.

All the girls looked from Marjorie to Francy. No one spoke. "I'm certainly glad my lunch doesn't come with ashes," Marjorie added, taking a sandwich from a shiny tin container built to fit into her new lunch pail.

Francy couldn't speak. The wonderful joy she'd felt over her new jumper evaporated. She sank into that same awful quicksand she had felt the Saturday her mother finished the drapes for Mrs. Douglas. After receiving payment, the family had gone shopping for school shoes. The children who couldn't fit into shoes outgrown by older children got a new pair. And each pupil got a paper tablet and two pencils. "Take care of these," said their father, "for they will have to do all year. Even

Santa Claus is broke this year."

Francy had looked quickly around Mr. MacDougal's store to see if anyone else had heard her father. She didn't mind doing without things, but she wanted her poverty kept private.

Under the cedars, Marjorie's giggles persisted and Francy hastily thrust the potato back in the plaid lunch bag her mother had sewn for her.

Conversation about other things began, and Marjorie munched happily on her sandwich.

After a few minutes Miss Faye knelt down by their group with her hand outstretched. "Look what I found on the tree I was resting on." The outer shell of a cicada stood statuelike on her palm.

"Ooooh, a bug," Marjorie shrieked, leaning away from the shell.

"Not a bug—a miracle," Miss Faye corrected. "It represents a change in the life of a living creature. It shows us how we all grow and change when we've outgrown our small, little worlds."

"We can't split our skin like a cicada," Wilma said.

"No, we can't," agreed Miss Faye with a smile. "But sometimes we outgrow our ideas and leave them behind. Especially if our ideas are small or unkind."

The girls studied the teacher's caring eyes and tried to understand.

"What a beautiful lunch bag!" Miss Faye said, reaching to pick up Francy's pouch. "Wherever did you find it?"

"My mother made it," she said, hoping her teacher would not ask about its contents.

"It's wonderful. And look at the drawstrings. Your mother is such a clever woman. So inventive," said Miss Faye. "I must have one just like it!"

Francy smiled nervously.

"I'll send Mrs. Ponder a note this afternoon. That is if you don't mind someone having the same bag."

"No," answered Francy quickly. "I don't mind."

"And look," said Miss Faye, reaching inside and lifting out the sweet potato, "my favorite lunch. My, my, my, this takes me back. My grandmother always packed these for me when I was in school. She said they were the healthiest thing a child could eat." She smiled at Francy and then at Marjorie. "I really must apologize. I was so busy admiring Francy's bag I've kept her from her lunch."

"It's all right. I really wasn't very hungry."

"Nonsense. But do you mind if I break off a little piece just for old time's sake?"

Francy nodded, too astonished for words.

As Miss Faye handed the potato back to Francy, the teacher dug deeper in the plaid sack and pulled out a biscuit and a small container of honeycomb. "Wild honey!" she exclaimed. "My, this bag has no end of wonders." She broke the biscuit in pieces and insisted that all the girls dip themselves a sticky treat.

Francy sat amazed as the others followed Miss Faye's lead in praising the wonders of her lunch.

Even Marjorie begged for a bit of the comb to chew after Miss Faye explained how the bees labor endlessly to change honey into beeswax.

However unkind Marjorie might have been, Francy couldn't thank her enough for kindling the great friendship Francy and Miss Faye shared from that day on.

"Life would be perfect," Francy admitted to Pauline on the walk home one afternoon, "if only we weren't so poor. I hear them talking at night when they think I'm asleep. They're worried about getting us through winter."

"I know," replied her sister. "I can't help overhearing them some nights. 'Don't worry; we'll manage.' That's what they always end up saying. So I guess we'll have to say it too."

Chapter 14

Since the beginning of the school year, Friday evenings had become the busiest time of the week. That was because Saturday was market day for the whole community. The Ponders would be going to town the next morning, and they wanted to be ready! The woodstove was heating kettle after kettle of water for baths, and the big kitchen was filled with steam.

"Be careful not to scald my babies," Mrs. Ponder warned, as Pauline poured hot water into the big tub where Jesse and Matthew splashed. Mrs. Ponder was giving Peter a haircut.

"Hot water's the only way to clean young rabbits," Pauline said, lathering the heads of the twins.

"I'll trade jobs with you any time," Francy said as she combed and twisted Eunice's freshly shampooed hair into curling pins.

"No thanks," said Pauline, who already wore a

head full of hairpins and clips. "We'd all come out looking like nine miles of tangled barbed wire. You've got the knack."

"Sure wish I'd lose it," Francy huffed.

"Mustn't think like that," their mother said patiently, as she dusted Peter's neck with talcum powder before moving on to Chester. "We're all blessed with talents. Be glad about sharing them." Her comb and shears worked in tandem. "Chet, hold still before I snip off an ear. Peter, get the broom and sweep up some of this hair."

"Francy's got it hard all right," Chet teased. "She doesn't have to chop all the wood to heat this bathwater or lug in bucket after bucket."

Francy made a face at her brother behind their mother's back.

"Ouch! Francy, you're pulling my hair out by the roots," Eunice complained.

"Sorry," she said, already parting the next strand to be pinned around her finger. Francy concentrated on her task, thinking of the happy time she would soon be having.

She knew that the well-groomed Ponder family would arrive in town by eleven o'clock the next morning to take care of the week's business. Francy loved the commotion of market day and visiting with friends and neighbors.

She was so happy with the thought that she could hardly manage to pout about having four more heads of hair to do at Cora's.

The next morning in town, Miss Faye greeted

them warmly at the post office. Francy blushed happily when the teacher praised her work to Mr. and Mrs. Ponder.

Francy blushed again at MacDougal's Mercantile, this time without any happiness at all. Mac accepted Mrs. Ponder's eggs and credited their account.

"Mrs. Ponder, Mr. Ponder," the shopkeeper began, "I'm sorrier than words can say. But you still owe. I know you're good folks and working hard . . ." He cleared his throat and dropped his eyes to his smudged apron. "But I just can't let out any more credit." He hurried to explain, "I'm carrying a good many folks as is and—"

"I understand," interrupted Mr. Ponder. "Times are hard. You've been a friend, Mac, and we'll be paying you as soon as we can. But the way things are, I'll make no promises."

"I hope you understand this isn't my doing," pleaded Mr. MacDougal. "I hate it; what with cold weather coming . . . and Christmas."

"Ease your mind," assured Mrs. Ponder. "We do understand. We're the lucky ones. We have food in the cellar, firewood at the mill, warm bedding, clothes, and enough shoe leather to last out the winter."

"Mrs. Ponder," Mac said with a quivering voice, "you're a fine lady."

"You'll get every egg my family can spare," continued their mother.

"And I'll deliver cordwood, till we get paid up," added Mr. Ponder.

Mac nodded his head.

"No butter or cheese to trade without Belle. But any sewing your family needs, you just let me know and we'll . . ."

Francy could listen no more. Saturday was supposed to be her day of pleasure. She escaped outside to the sidewalk, staring vacantly at the shop windows.

"Well, Francy Ponder, aren't you gonna say hello?" came the gruff voice. Francy looked up into the face of Mrs. Trundle.

The two were still talking when her mother finally came out of the store. "How good to see you," greeted Mae Ponder. "Why aren't you feeding people at the boarding house?"

"No boarders; and the locals are too broke to buy a slice of bread."

Hearing the community sharing their poverty made Francy feel better, but only for a moment.

"Times are lean all over," her mother added.

Francy wanted to run away before the humiliation started again. But the two women talked for what seemed like hours, exposing the poorness of the country, the town, and—to Francy's horror—of the Ponders.

"No getting around it," said Mrs. Trundle. "Everyone's in the same boat—and barely afloat."

"Even Santa's poor this year," sighed Mrs. Ponder.

"No doubt," replied Mrs. Trundle.

"Excuse me," interrupted Francy, "but I'd better

get up to Cora's and start setting hair." She marched along Piney's slanty sidewalks, kicking any litter that came close to her foot. The sky no longer seemed a brilliant blue, and the colorful leaves on the trees and the ground no longer seemed so beautiful. "I hate being poor," she complained to herself. "And I hate all this talk of Santa Claus being poor."

Instead of going in Cora's front door as she usually did, Francy circled to the rear of the house planning to visit Belle. She could hear Marjorie's shrill voice even before she swung open the stable door.

Francy's heart jumped up in her throat when she saw Marjorie, pitchfork in hand, jabbing its prongs just inches from Belle's terrified face. The gentle Jersey pulled back as far as her halter would permit, and her eyes were wild with fear.

Marjorie was screaming, "You stupid cow! I hate you! I hate cleaning up after you! Because of you I have to spend my Saturday cleaning manure! I hate you!"

Francy grabbed the pitchfork and threw it down before Marjorie ever knew anyone was behind her. She pushed Belle's tormentor hard against the wall of the stable.

"If you ever mistreat Belle again . . ." Francy paused, trying to think of a strong enough threat.

"Don't tell me how to treat my own cow!" Marjorie screamed. "She's not yours anymore! You're family's too poor to even keep a cow! You may be Miss High-and-Mighty Teacher's Pet at school, Francy Ponder, but you're poorer than dirt! So don't come round here on your high horse trying to boss . . ."

Marjorie paused as Francy took a step closer, with fire in her eyes. Suddenly, Marjorie's arrogant face lost its smug grimace and turned white.

Francy had never been so angry. Marjorie was scared of her now and Francy was glad. She wanted Marjorie to have the same wild-eyed fear she'd seen a moment ago on Belle's face.

"Marjorie, go into the house," Mrs. Ponder commanded sternly from the doorway. "Go this instant!"

Marjorie was glad to obey and quickly flew out of the stable.

Without a word, Mrs. Ponder hugged Francy to her side, and the two of them slowly approached the poor cow and gently stroked her forehead.

Francy set no hair at Cora's that Saturday. And after church on Sunday Mrs. Ponder brought Belle home. All but a small portion of the milk was delivered daily to Cora's. But it was always sent with Peter or Chester. No mention was ever made of who owned Belle or how long she would stay. Ponders, both young and old, petted the animal like a long-lost sister. And if a cow *can* look grateful, Belle did.

Chapter 15

"You need to see a dentist."

Francy could hear her parents arguing from her bedroom.

"Can't afford it."

"But . . ."

"That's all, Mae. A bad tooth never killed anyone. There's no money."

"There may not be money." Francy could hear her mother's protest. "But this tooth's paining you something fierce. Cheeks puffed out like a chipmunk with an acorn. This clove oil is no solution."

"Helps a spell," said Francy's father. "And that's all the help there is right now."

An icy snake coiled up in Francy's stomach and sent shivers up her back as she listened to her parents. The big rock house felt like a fortress against harm, but Francy knew it was her parents' courage that made life seem happy and secure.

By the middle of October, Francy no longer looked forward to their Saturday visits to town. Each trip to MacDougal's Mercantile ended with her parents explaining, "This year even Santa Claus is poor. Don't be expecting too much this Christmas."

One Saturday, Francy could not take her eyes from a lady's manicure kit resting in MacDougal's showcase. Shaped like a small book, it was covered with magenta velvet on the outside and black satin within. There were leather loops neatly holding the tiny scissors, the pearl-handled nail file, and six other shiny tools. The edges of the set were bound in wide strips of gold with a golden clasp that clicked open and shut. For a brief moment Francy daydreamed about giving the elegant kit to her mother on Christmas morning.

But daydreams vanished when shoppers started talking about an impoverished Santa Claus.

As she held a squirming toddler by each hand, Francy wondered what sort of Christmas it would be.

Her father interrupted her thoughts by scooping a twin up on either shoulder. "Let's walk over to Blake Wylie's mill."

They crossed the town of Piney in silence, Francy still fretting over thoughts of the coming holiday.

"Francy, did I ever tell you about my old cat Samson?" her father asked, breaking the silence and the frown on his daughter's face.

"No."

"Well, Samson . . ."

"Does this story have anything to do with Santa?" Francy asked.

"Not a thing!" her father laughed.

"Good."

"Well, Samson . . ."

". . . about being broke?"

"Not that either."

"Good!"

"Well, Samson fooled us from the very first," her father explained. "He turned out to be a girl. Not a pretty, fluffy cat—Samson was rawbones and slick-haired. But smart!" Will whistled. "That was the smartest cat ever to come down the pike."

"Smart as Fluffy and Sugar?"

"Smarter. I was about your age, Francy, and your grandma had me weeding the garden in early spring. Old Samson had had herself a litter of kittens out under the shed. She wouldn't let a soul close enough to count 'em. Every time we tried, she'd up and move the babies."

"What's so smart about that?" Francy asked impatiently.

"Well, Francy, I looked up from my weeding and saw old Samson coming across the meadow. She was moving so slow I thought she was stuck in a trap or something. But she kept on coming."

Jesse and Matthew squirmed until their father set them down to walk beside him.

"Lickety split I run back to the house yelling, 'Ma! Ma, come quick!' Ma flew out the door, drying her hands on her apron and expecting something awful. I told her, 'Old Samson's been fishing.'

"'Heavens above, child,' she said. 'I thought your brother had surely fallen down the well, and you drag me away from my work to tell me a cat's caught a fish.'

"'No, Ma,' I cried. 'Miss Samson hasn't caught a fish. She's toting in a whole stringer of fish.'

"Well, ma followed me, her long skirts trailing over the meadow grass. Sure enough that cat was dragging the prettiest mess of bluegill and goggle-eye fish you'd ever want to see. Stringer got caught on weeds every little bit. Then Samson would yank it loose and keep on tugging."

"Oh, Pa," scolded Francy. "How could a cat thread fish on a stringer?"

"I'm only telling what I saw with my own two eyes. 'Isn't that just the berries?' my Ma said. 'Ain't that just the berries?'"

"My family laughed and joked for years about having the smartest cat in Carston County."

The story ended just as they arrived at Blake Wylie's mill. Francy entertained the twins outside while their father went inside with Blake.

Francy was just thinking how nothing smelled as good as fresh sawdust when their father reappeared holding his old red bandanna wadded in his fist.

"What's that?" Jesse asked.

"Guess."

After several minutes of letting Matthew and Jesse guess, Mr. Ponder unwrapped the cloth. Inside was the tooth that had given him so much trouble.

Chapter 16

It was late October. The oil lamps burned brightly as everyone did school work at the long table.

Mrs. Ponder pulled her rocker nearer the light and unfolded *The Weekly Prospect*. Mr. Ponder sat nearby mending shoes. Occasionally, Mae would read some article of news aloud. The twins crawled under the long table, tickling everyone's feet and then laughing as if they had just played the world's greatest joke.

Suddenly, Mae stood straight up out of her rocker and walked to the table, where the lamp's light was brightest.

Francy was the first to catch the look on her mother's face. She stopped writing, knowing something important was about to happen.

"Listen to this," Mrs. Ponder said, never lifting her eyes from the paper.

"What is it?" they all asked.

"I'll read it: *Wanted: Black walnut kernels, 25 cents per pound, quick payment guaranteed, Forester Candy Company, Chicago.*"

"Black walnuts?" all the Ponders asked.

"Black walnuts!" they cheered at once, realizing the significance of the ad. There was so much happy jabbering that soon Jesse and Matthew were squealing with delight and clapping their hands.

Nuts were one thing the family was rich in. The ad might just as easily have offered to trade gold dust for the mountain of sawdust behind Mr. Ponder's mill.

The rest of the evening was a celebration, with big bowls of popcorn perfuming the air, youngsters swinging each other round and round the kitchen, and their parents laying plans that could earn real money to pay debts and maybe even save Christmas.

The thirty-foot boat that Will had built, but never sold, had been dry-docked under the elms in the yard. Every afternoon the children returned from school to find that bushels of walnuts had been dumped into the boat. And every night the miraculous plan to save Christmas unfolded further.

After dishes and chores, the children settled down to school work and their parents settled down to cracking and hulling black walnuts. As the children finished their studies, they were allowed to help. The younger ones were simply to sort the large kernels from the small, and to take out any stray shells that found their way into the precious cargo.

Usually each night, Mrs. Ponder would stop picking nuts long enough to read aloud from whatever book she'd gotten from the library. However, tonight was something special. Tonight there was a letter from Elly.

As in most Ozark homes, mail delivery was an occasion. But when it brought an envelope post-marked *New York City*, it meant news from Francy's spunky half sister, as well as a few dollars to help the family through these difficult times. Elly worked as a maid in New York. Her letters described life in the city. But best of all there was always a special note to each of the Ponder children. Francy's paragraph read:

> *Francy, I wish you could come for a visit. New York has so much to see. I work in a home larger than any building in Piney. Bigger even than MacDougal's Mercantile. Your sweeping and dusting would be a big help. I keep the second floor—there are four floors all together. Everything is so beautiful you don't really mind tending to it. I have several friends—and one enemy—among the others girls working here. Mostly folks are nice. But I miss the hills and my little freckled sister.*

Preparing the nuts always seemed easier when Mrs. Ponder read to them. Even though they were a long way from their goal, the whole family seemed lighthearted when they remembered the wonderful ad in the *Prospect* and how it was going to save the holidays.

Chapter 17

Days grew shorter and colder, and the wondrous jars that had filled the cellar decreased at an alarming rate.

Mrs. Ponder's sewing machine was kept busy mending and remaking garments for the family.

Mr. Ponder's job was harder. He constantly mended holes in the soles of the children's shoes.

With great hope, the family gathered nightly to pursue their great money-earning project. Every night was a contest to see how many nuts could be cracked and sorted in the course of a single evening. Sometimes their mother would read aloud to them as they worked; sometimes their father would lead them in singing. Sunday was the only day the project was put aside.

"Today's the day," Mrs. Ponder whispered to the children over breakfast. "Last night your father weighed the nuts. We've shelled forty-five pounds according to the scale. And the scale hasn't been used for much in years, so we're sending extra for good measure."

The children helped to sort and reweigh the nuts a second and third time, carefully bundling them according to the ad's instructions. A few pennies were pilfered from the egg money for postage, and the parcel was sent—along with the family's dreams—to the candy company in Chicago. Speedy payment had been promised in the paper and was eagerly awaited by the family.

Every afternoon when Mr. Dowd's rickety truck rattled to a stop at their mailbox, Mae Ponder was at the gate.

"Howdy, Mr. Dowd. Only accepting good news today."

"Howdy, Miz Ponder," the weathered mail carrier replied, sorting through his mail pouch. "Really enjoyed your quartet at church last Sunday."

"Thank you. Is this all?"

"Yep. All today."

The Forester Candy Company was not as prompt as the Ponders had hoped, but they began working immediately on their second shipment.

"No sense wasting time," their father joked after supper. "Practice makes perfect."

"Well, we'll soon be the champions," laughed Pauline.

"I thought picking cotton was hard on your hands," Peter complained. "But these nuts wear the skin clear off your fingers."

"Stop your squawking, Peter," Francy said. "Next fair we'll set up a nut-picking event. See which family in the county can pick and sort the most nuts in half an hour."

Everyone laughed at the thought.

"Of course, we'll win. We'll be professionals by then."

"Our fingers will have calluses so we can endure the pain."

"We'll surely win first prize," Chester said.

"Which will probably be more nuts!" Eunice laughed.

The nights went on with the family pursuing their great campaign. Mrs. Ponder would read a chapter or two. Sometimes everyone worked in silence, and Francy imagined spending the money a dozen different ways, visions of Christmas gifts and treats dancing in her head.

The first Saturday of December there was no trip to Piney. Peter and Chester went with their father to deliver firewood to two families—one paying in cornmeal and the other with molasses.

It was warm for December, and Francy talked to the hens as she gathered the eggs and filled feed trays. "How do you like my hair? I curled four heads of hair last night, and now we don't even get to go to town. At least Belle thought I looked elegant when I milked her this morning."

Francy heard a truck rattling up the gravel road as she walked back with the eggs. "This must be the day," Francy whispered, leaving the egg basket on the porch. "Maybe I'll be glad I didn't go to Piney."

Francy was by the gate when Mr. Dowd's dust-covered truck came to a stop.

"Howdy, Miz Francy," the old man said, searching through his pouch.

"Afternoon, Mr. Dowd."

"Expectin' somethin' special?"

"Might be," Francy said, accepting the mail through the truck's open window.

"Hope it's in there."

"Thank you," Francy replied, her hands already sorting through the envelopes as the truck rattled off.

"Oh, my!" Francy took off at a full run, charging into the house.

"Mama! Mama! Mama!" she screamed, bringing Mrs. Ponder from her sewing room and everyone else from various parts of the house. "It's here! It's here! Mr. Dowd just delivered it!"

Everyone waited breathless. Mrs. Ponder looked at the insignia of the Forester Candy Company printed on the envelope. Her nimble fingers ripped it open.

Francy and her sisters stood frozen as Mrs. Ponder read. They were still as statues when the tears silently slid down the face of their mother, the woman who had been so brave and hopeful throughout all the hard times. Even after she disappeared into her bedroom, they could hear the sobs she tried to muffle in her pillow.

That was enough for the twins, who began

75

crying tears of their own and sobbing, "Mama, Mama."

"Mama has a bad headache," Eunice said, lifting Jesse. "Let's take a walk and give her a little quiet so she'll feel better."

Pauline lifted Matthew.

Francy picked up the check, noticing its small amount. She read aloud, *"Dear Mrs. Ponder: We are enclosing . . ."* She scanned ahead: *"Your nuts were inspected and graded fourth class. . . . In addition, there were shells found in an inspection sample, and accordingly you were docked ten cents a pound . . ."*

"Those dirty liars," Pauline whispered. "There wasn't a sliver of a shell in the whole bunch. Why, we sifted through every . . ."

"Girls," interrupted Eunice, "let's take the twins. Mama needs time alone."

Walking the twins gave the girls a chance to talk.

"Those candy people are liars. We picked every shell out of those nuts—even the fine slivers," Pauline said, kicking rocks as she walked along.

Eunice added, "And the nerve of grading our nuts fourth class when every one of them was fresh and firm."

"I'd just like to tell them a thing or two!"

"That's not what's important now!" Francy, who had been walking along in silence, almost shouted.

Everyone stopped in their tracks and stared at their youngest sister. "Mama's hurt. She almost died of that fever, but it never made her give up. Mama has faith. She never gives in. But these candy folks have made her give up hope." Francy stopped for breath. "What's important now—right now—is how to stop Mama's heart from breaking. We've got to plan—and plan quickly."

"She's right," Eunice admitted.

So while strolling the rocky hills, the girls planned to take away the bitter sting of the Forester Candy Company's empty promises.

Chapter 18

That evening Francy managed to warn her father and brothers of the letter before they got to the house. After Francy's explanation, everyone entered the house as if nothing were awry. No one moaned about the disappointment or even acted as if they'd ever heard of black walnuts.

Eunice had fixed a special dinner with two peach cobblers for dessert. And when their father went in to get their mother, they all held their breath as they finished setting the table.

The family tried its best to keep up the conversation during dinner. Peter told of seeing a dog with one brown eye and one blue eye.

"You never seen the like," Chester added between bites. "Looked like a good hunting dog, but never barked or howled or bayed. Nothing at all."

Their mother passed dishes but never said a word or ate a bite.

When the usual time came to prepare nuts, everyone found other things to do. There was no mention of the dashed hopes that had hinged on the project.

Everyone did his or her chores without being asked. When Eunice and Pauline began to bicker over whose turn it was to trim the lamp wicks in the sitting room, Francy quickly said, "I'll do it." When Peter and Chester began to discuss who should get more wood for the stove, Francy said, "I'll get it." If any of the Ponder children even thought of being disagreeable, Francy's quick example reminded them to be cheerful and considerate.

Chapter 19

It was the week before Christmas. No snow had fallen, but a heavy frost lay on the ground. "Brrrrrr," Francy said, setting the steaming milk pail on the back porch to cool. "I had to warm my hands before Belle would let me touch her."

"Looks like a fine day to cut lumber," her father said, his hands wrapped around a mug of coffee.

Peter and Chester moaned, thinking of standing for hours in the toe-numbing cold while feeding logs into the saw.

"It's Saturday," Peter complained. "Aren't we going to town?"

"We can't be going out in this weather," Eunice replied. "The twins have a cough. Sound like a pair of lovesick bullfrogs."

"I've bundled them up," Francy added. "But they're in for the day."

"And I rubbed their chests with camphorated oil," Pauline added.

"You're good nurses," Peter said. "We'll tell you all about town as soon as we get back."

"Yeah," Chester added, "we'll tell the *girls* all the news soon as we get back."

"What about you, Mae?" Mr. Ponder asked. "Do you want to go to Piney?"

"No," their mother said flatly, as she stirred gravy for the biscuits in the oven. "There's not a single thing in town we need. Or that we can afford."

"Good," Will said. "Then you'll have no objections if I take the boys out to the log woods."

Peter groaned.

"I thought we already had more timber than we could sell," Chester said.

"Well," their father teased, "that blanket of frost put me in the mood to cut just one more tree."

"A Christmas tree!" Pauline squealed, her golden braids flying out as she turned quickly to see her father's grin.

Francy did not squeal. She tried hard not to let the disappointment of having no decorations show.

Jesse and Matthew, who looked like tightly wrapped dolls in the old trundle bed behind the stove, began to squeal, too. "Twis'mus twee! Twis'mus twee!"

After breakfast, the Ponder men disappeared, and Mrs. Ponder checked on the twins before climbing the stairs to her sewing room to finish Francy's angel costume for the Christmas pageant.

"She spends too much time up there these days," Francy said, passing the platter she had just washed to Pauline to rinse and dry.

Francy would have liked to have disappeared into her own room for the day. The look on her mother's face the day that dreadful check arrived still haunted her. So without a word she carried in several armloads of wood and fed it into the stove.

"What are you doing? You're going to roast the twins if you keep adding wood!" Eunice said.

"Now that you mention it they do look like two plump little lambs. But the answer's no. I'm not interested in roasting them but in popping corn."

Her sisters quickly caught on to Francy's idea and helped her pop pan after pan of popcorn.

Stringing the corn took the three sisters all the rest of the morning and afternoon. They worked even between preparations for the evening meal. Francy put on her coat and began carrying in more wood.

"What's all this?" Eunice asked, feeding the twins a molasses biscuit. "We've already popped all the corn. I'm almost blind from stringing so much."

"We're going to bake."

"Bake?" said Pauline. "Bake what?"

"Cookies, of course," answered Francy. "We've got almost fifteen pounds of nuts picked. Can't let them go to waste."

The aroma of black-walnut cookies had filled the house by the time Mr. Ponder and the boys returned. Her brothers greedily gobbled some cookies. Then they brought in the cedar that had been carefully chosen for the corner of the front room.

"Nice tree," Francy said, noticing how large it was and how hopeless decorating even a third of it would be.

Then Francy had an idea. Quickly she found some colored paper in the cedar chest. Everyone, even the twins, sat at the kitchen table cutting and pasting a long chain to wrap around the Christmas tree.

"I'll do all the outside chores," their father said. "You need plenty of time to decorate a tree as big as this."

It was growing late when the children finished their decorating. Mrs. Ponder emerged from the stairway carrying a stack of boxes, which she dramatically placed on a stool near the tree. "You boys picked a real beauty," she said. "And the popcorn and colored chains look beautiful."

With that she lifted the lid off one of the boxes.

"Ooooooh!" gasped the children as they looked inside. The box was filled with upholstered Christmas balls the size of large apples. There were spheres of teal blue brocade from the Douglases' drapes, and balls of gold tapestry from Miss Whittier's high-backed dining chairs. But the two toddlers couldn't take their chubby hands off the globes of deep scarlet velvet, fashioned from remnants of the new stage curtains in the school auditorium.

"Now we know what you've been up to in your sewing room," Francy said. "Making all these must have kept you up nights."

Her mother smiled. "Necessity is the mother of invention."

The children happily got busy. Soon all the balls were hung. The brothers and sisters stood around the tree admiring their work.

"Who'd like to help me open this box?" their mother asked.

After everyone had volunteered, they decided that the twins should have the honor. "Oooooh," the twins said, their mouths in perfect little circles.

The second box held bows made from the richest fabrics in the county. And the third box contained keepsakes from past Christmases, along with several birds' nests and dozens of wooden spools decorated with lace, ribbons, and sequins.

"My stars!" Mr. Ponder exclaimed, returning from the evening chores. "Whoever would have thought that the tree we brought home would turn out like this!"

No one noticed their mother's absence as they stood admiring the tree, until she returned carrying a five-pointed patchwork star stuffed with soft cotton. Each point was sewn in two shades of satin and outlined in gold braid.

"It's beautiful!" gasped Pauline.

"Climb up, Papa," Francy said, carrying in a kitchen chair. "Climb up and put the star on our tree."

Will Ponder balanced on the chair and his wife handed him the star. He stretched to reach the top of the tree.

"Careful now."

"Higher."

"All the way up."

"A little more to the right."

"It's crooked. Tilt it a little ways back."

"How about now?"

"It's perfect! It's lovely! It's absolutely perfect!" everyone shouted.

After the evening meal, the family hurried to the front room, where the wood stove greeted them with its warmth. The wicks of the kerosene lamps were trimmed without a hint of bickering over whose turn it was.

All the Ponders sat admiring the tree.

After everyone had watched in silence for a long time, Mr. Ponder spoke. "It's the most beautiful tree I've ever seen. Fit for a king."

"Most beautiful tree in the whole world," Peter added. "And I chopped it down."

"It's Mama's star that makes it so special," said Pauline.

"And the smocked balls."

"And the bows."

"No doubt about it," Chester said proudly. "We have the most glorious tree in Missouri and probably in the United States of America and maybe in the world."

"Let's not get too high and mighty," their mother said. She held the twins on her lap, quietly rocking them near the warmth of the woodstove.

Chapter 20

And so Christmas came even without the aid of the Forester Candy Company.

Mrs. Trundle stopped by with a large pan of hot rolls. "I always fix too much dough," she explained. "I'm useless when it comes to fixing for just a few." Upon entering the front room, she stopped as if rooted to the spot. Finally she spoke. "In all my seventy-six years, I've never seen the like. Why, it's a miracle. Mae Ponder, you sly fox. What a Christmas tree!"

After Mrs. Trundle's visit, news spread fast. Everyone seemed to find a reason to pay a visit to the Ponders.

Francy's heart soared like a bird each time neighbors stopped by to see the tree. There were plenty of Francy's black-walnut cookies to share, and everyone raved about Mrs. Ponder's black-walnut applesauce cake.

When Maude, Marjorie, and Miriam came by the day before Christmas Eve, Francy felt a warm joy filling her entire body. Cora's girls were not only astonished at the sight of the tree, they were awestruck. For once there was complete silence upon their arrival. The Ponders all stood still, holding their breath, to see how long the spell would last.

After what seemed several minutes, the visitors looked at one another and began to cry. Then a mighty racket filled the house all the way to its rafters.

"Why can't we ever have beautiful ornaments on our tree?" Marjorie wailed.

"Our tree is so ugly!" Maude cried, jumping up and down and stamping her feet.

Miriam, imitating her sisters, stamped her feet and cried. "Our tree! Our tree!" she shouted, pointing at the beautiful cedar.

Francy felt guilty about enjoying the three-ring spectacle in their front room. Try as she might, she couldn't muster up a crumb of sympathy for Cora, who held her aching forehead and lamely apologized, "We'll get nice ornaments."

Miriam stamped her feet so hard, the ornaments danced on the green boughs.

"We'll have Gran'Mae help us. You'll help us, won't you, Mae? We'll have the nicest tree ever."

Maude wailed louder and louder.

"Yes, yes, darlings, I hear you. We'll have the most beautiful tree in the county and then . . ."

"Enough!" Jake shouted at last. "Enough is enough!" His booming shout rose up through the ranting of the tantrum.

The room grew quiet. No one had ever heard Jake raise his voice.

Finally Cora stammered, "Now, Jake, the girls . . ."

"Enough!" He said more quietly, but just as firmly. "Girls, keep your coats on and get back in the car."

"Jake," Cora protested.

"In the car, girls! Right now!" He turned toward the assembled Ponders. "I apologize for our behavior," Jake said, tipping his hat. "We'll come visiting again as soon as we've learned a few manners."

The door closed. No one spoke. Everyone gazed at the tree as if the scene that had just unfolded might be a dream. They remained quiet even after the sound of the Model A died away.

Chester finally spoke very softly. "Look, it's starting to snow."

Chapter 21

On Christmas Eve, Chet Dowd, the mail carrier, brought the mail all the way to the door.

"Come in! Come in, Mr. Dowd, before you freeze," Eunice welcomed.

"Don't mind if I do. I'm cold as the dickens. Been pushin' old Nellie out of drifts all over Carston County." He stomped the snow off his boots before stepping inside. "Howdy, Miz Ponder."

"Sit a spell, Mr. Dowd," Mae encouraged, pushing her rocker right next to the stove.

"Brought you a package. Good tidings, I hope."

"We thank you for carrying it clean to the house," Mrs. Ponder said. "Pauline, bring a cup of hot coffee for Mr. Dowd."

Francy crowded close to the rocker as the old man rubbed his hands together near the stove. Clues to where the package had come from were hidden by his coat.

"Mind your manners, Francy," her mother warned.

Blushing, Francy backed away.

"It's all right." Mr. Dowd smiled. "Most ever'one needs to peek at something once in a while. Why, I walked this package up to the house just so's I could sneak a peek at this here tree." His grin grew even bigger as he leaned back in the rocker, took a sip of the steaming mug of coffee, and studied the cedar. "Heard about it clean over to Tyler. Had to see for myself. Danged if it ain't better than folks say."

Then he handed the box to Francy and the envelopes to Pauline. "Merry Christmas!" he said, heading toward the door.

"Same to you!" Mrs. Ponder said, as the old man pulled down his earflaps and shoved his hands back in his gloves. "Tree or not, you're always welcome. Come in and warm yourself, mail or no mail."

"It's from Elly," Francy announced upon Mr. Dowd's departure. "Let's open it."

"Easy does it," their mother said, sitting in the rocker and placing the box on her lap. "That's Elly's writing all right. Heavy, too."

The box was opened, revealing dozens of smaller packages wrapped in red and green paper and labeled "Do Not Open Till Christmas."

Each present passed through eager fingers until their mother announced, "It's time to be getting ready for the pageant. You all put the packages under the tree now."

Leaving those beautiful packages with Elly's fine

labeling was like smelling gingerbread and not being allowed to taste it.

Francy's angel costume was the best one, and none of the children forgot a single one of their lines. A gentle snow was falling when they left the church for the ride home. The twins fell asleep on their mother's lap. The rest of the children were bundled up in the back of the lumber truck enjoying the quiet beauty of the snow-covered forest.

Chapter 22

"Wake up, Jesse! Wake up, Matthew!" said Francy. "It's Christmas. It's Christmas morning."

Mr. Ponder had such a fire blazing in the front room that even barefooted children in nightgowns and flannel pajamas didn't feel the morning's chill.

"Gather round for cocoa," Mrs. Ponder said, carrying in a tray of steaming cups. "This is Belle's special Christmas present to each and every one of us."

They sipped their creamy cocoa and munched black-walnut cookies. One by one, they opened each package, enjoying the glory of the moment as long as possible.

When Cora and Jake's family arrived for Christmas dinner, Francy was in such a fine mood that she only smiled and said, "Why, that's grand," when Marjorie showed her the beautiful velvet manicure set she had received.

And to Francy's surprise, she found no lump in her throat or ache in her heart when Marjorie said, "You can look, but do not touch."

For it had dawned on Francy while opening the gifts that this would always be her special Christmas. All the Christmas mornings in her life to come would make her remember this day. The memory of the same regal cedar chopped down by her brothers, of her parents kissing under the mistletoe, of cookies made with black walnuts that were never sent to market, and more than anything else, of this family—her family!

It was on this special Christmas morning that Francy understood the secret revealed only to the wisest: *Christmas is not at all about the presents we receive. It's about sharing ourselves with those we love.*

Chapter 23

"Being duped by the candy company was no tragedy," Francy would tell her own children years later. "It was a blessing. It sparked our excitement for better times ahead. But most important it made us appreciate all that we already had that Christmas day. We had Mama healthy again. We had Papa working hard to keep our family together. We had Belle—she might not have belonged to us, but she never left home again. We had each other, squabbling like all brothers and sisters do, but also precious to one another. And after Jake took a hand with the girls, Marjorie and I became the best of friends.

"Yes, it was a country Christmas—one to remember!"

🍒 Francy's Country Cookies 🍒

1 cup (.24 l) white sugar
1 cup (.24 l) brown sugar
1 cup (.24 l) shortening
2 eggs, beaten
4 cups (1 l) flour
4 teaspoons (20 ml) baking powder
1/2 cup (.12 l) sweet milk*
1 teaspoon (5 ml) vanilla
1 cup (.24 l) oats
1 cup (.24 l) black walnuts, chopped

Preheat oven to 350°F (176°C).

Cream together sugars and shortening and add beaten eggs. Sift flour and baking powder together and add to shortening mixture along with milk and vanilla. Stir in oats and nuts. Mixture will be stiff.

Drop teaspoons of dough onto cookie sheets. Flatten slightly with a floured fork.

Place in preheated oven and bake 12 minutes.

NOTE: Cookie size may be varied. Adjust baking time accordingly.

YIELD: Approximately 4 dozen cookies.

*Sweet milk is an old term for milk. (It is not buttermilk or soured milk.)